ABOUT THE AUTHOR

Maria Jeo. Is the Senior Executive in charge of Operations and Security in a reputable organization, overseeing informational technology and other bank support services. She has nearly three decades of financial operations experience, and has served at SNB since 1992.

She is also an author of over 8 books all related to best ways to identify a romance scammer and it's preventive measures.

TABLE OF CONTENT

INTRODUCTION

Eeach year thousands of Americans who are searching for love end up with nothing but a broken heart and an empty wallet.

An increasing number of Americans are becoming victims of romance scams, mostly originating from West Africa.

Romance scams, also known as confidence scams, result in the highest amount of financial losses when compared to other Internet-facilitated crimes. In this book I will be revealing to you lies romance scammer tell. I also recommend my books especially "14 Warning Signs Your Prince Charming Is Actually A Catfish & Scammer and Romance Scams and safety" the contents are very rich and will help you.

Chapter One

How To Outsmart A Romance Scammer: 13 Tips

Romance scammers have found their victims easier in today's digital age. Stealing a few of someone else's pictures is all it takes to create a new online persona. Dating websites are plush with potential victims.

Some scammers are so patient they don't mind waiting to gain your trust before taking you for everything you've ever had. This type of fraud is more common than most people think.

How To Avoid Becoming Prey To Romance Scammers: 13 Tips To Make Sure You're Not A Victim

Romance scammers come from every country, in every language, and from a variety of educational backgrounds. It could be the person that is well-spoken who claims to be a doctor. A seemingly innocent person that says they were just looking for friends on Facebook could also be a romance scammer.

Romance scams are the most common form of fraud today. While you can't always pinpoint whether a person is one or not, in the beginning, there are a few things you can do to avoid becoming a victim. Avoiding certain things can make you less likely to be a potential prey for them, too.

1. Don't post too much personal information online

Romance scammers will carefully read your profile. They absorb public information and use it against you. If you like heavy metal, they love it. They make sure that they seem perfectly in sync with you in order to gain your trust. This is just one of the popular tactics that they use to commit fraud.

You can avoid this by not posting too much personal information to the public. For example, avoid posting your address, phone number, financial information, or favorite things. If you're using a dating website, only put a few of your favorite things in your profile if others can see them. Save the rest of the details about yourself for those awesome getting to know you conversations.

2. Give yourself rules on social media sites

Social media sites are packed with con artists just like online dating sites. Don't accept friend requests from people you don't know. Limit public information about yourself to help deter a potential scammer.

3. Beware of an online romance

If someone is only interested in an online romance, that's a red flag that they are a scammer. These people will pretend to be someone they are not. Once you've taken the bait, they'll attempt the scam of the century.

4. Never send money

The entire point of online scams is for them to get in your pocket. A scammer will tell victims that they want a relationship. They could even be great at romance. This is all just a part of their game. It is designed to help earn your trust, even if it takes time to do that.

Then, once they have, they'll ask for money. It could be for an emergency. People that live in a different country will say that they need money to come to see you. Then, they never arrive. The emergencies never stop. This is because it's all a scam. To avoid falling victim to scams like this, never send money to someone you haven't met in person.

5. Beware of people that ask for money

A romance scammer will ultimately want money. That's the entire point behind a romance scam. This is one of the biggest red flags to watch out for to avoid romance scams. Personally, I have a rule that I won't give anyone money that I am not in a committed, personal relationship with.

It's important to note that romance scams don't usually involve outright asking a person for money. Instead, it's a process that involves online dating. There is romance. Then, they'll ask for money for a crisis. It pulls on your heartstrings.

Perhaps a loved one is in the hospital or dying. If you love children, the loved one will more than likely be a child. Romance scams will usually pull on your heartstrings because that's an easier way to get money.

6. Do an image search

A quick way to avoid a romance scam, and catch a scammer in their tracks, is by doing an online image search. If you're into online dating, do this when you're considering something more serious with someone, especially if you haven't met them in person.

To do an image search, you copy the person's image. You can then search other places for the picture online. If it shows up as someone else's profile picture on Facebook or under a different name, it could be a romance scam.

7. Never give out financial details

When someone is interested in dating and romance, financial details shouldn't come into play for quite a while. They shouldn't be discussed until at least both of you are considering a relationship.

For example, it's normal to talk about where you work out

in a budding romance. People that are dating might discuss buying things they're excited about, such as a new stand-up mixer or planning a vacation.

However, the small parts like how much you make per hour, how much your bonus was, or how much is in your savings account should not be relevant. If the person your talking to is insistent on finding out this information, it could be a dating scam.

8. Video chat

If they stole pictures from someone else, or their complete identity, they won't be able to video chat. This will be a dead giveaway that they are not who they said they were.

People that stole an identity from someone else also won't want to video chat because they have to keep up with their online persona, and it's harder to do that when you're talking compared to when you're texting.

If it's a scam, they won't come out right and tell you that they are looking for fresh victims. Instead, you are going to get a plethora of excuses. Their camera is broken. They don't have a good signal. The excuses won't stop, and you'll never be able to video chat if they are using a fake identity.

9. They fall in love quickly

Where it would normally take weeks, people in romance scams fall in love in a matter of days. They get to know you quickly. You'll hear that they've never felt like this about someone else, even though they've been in the online dating world for years. It's all a sign of a romance scam.

The person behind these scams is hoping that a woman will fall in love just as quickly, and then send them money.

Is it like pulling teeth getting him to spend time with you?

The key to solving is understanding men on a much deeper emotional level. The number #1 factor that causes men to behave this way is actually relatively easy to change with a few subtle things you can say to him.

Watch this free video that explains how you can become his priority!

10. They live overseas for now

A common theme behind romance scams is that they are from the U.S. and have to live overseas for now. The reasons for them living in another country may vary. Some people behind scams will say it's because they are taking care of a loved one. Another is that they are in the military.

11. Ask them for a picture doing something specific

Maybe they've got twenty pictures of them doing military things. Perhaps they also stole all twenty of those pictures. If something feels off or you want to make sure that someone is real, ask them for a very specific picture. For example, a picture of them holding up just their pinky. Or balancing a spoon on their nose.

Most people don't have pictures doing those things on a social media site, so it's unlikely a person behind a dating site scam will be able to follow through. (I do this with all military people because I have to deal with one potential scam after another.)

12. They are quick to move off of a dating site

When someone is behind a scam, they don't want to keep sending messages on a site. They want to move off the site even faster than they fall in love. This is because you can't report them to the site. Also, if you give them your email address or phone number it can give the person behind the scam access to more of your personal information.

If you move off a site, use a messaging app like KIK instead of giving out personal information.

13. Double-check spelling and grammar mistakes

We all make mistakes when we're typing or talking to people. However, if someone is from the United States, and claims that they were born in the United States, they should not be speaking in broken English. Make sure that their spelling and grammar mistakes make sense.

If they don't you can trust that they aren't being entirely truthful, which is one of the biggest signs of a romance scam.

Chapter Two

How can you tell if someone is a romance scammer?

Romance scams are typically seen in online dating. They fall in love quickly, don't like talking on the site, and then need money for something. Usually, it will be a family emergency, such as a loved one being sick. They don't meet up in person.

Do romance scammers video call?

Sometimes. Romance scammers might video chat with you, but they might not. It depends on whether they are pretending to be someone else. If they are using a different photo, they won't. Scammers that are using their real picture won't mind a video chat with their latest victim.

How do you spot a con artist in a relationship?

A con artist will move as fast as any other scammer. They call their victim a pet name sooner, fall in love quickly and the relationship moves along faster than any other one. It won't take long for the scammer to try and get personal information from their victim, like bank account info.

How do you beat a scammer?

Don't become a victim. Never give out personal information, like bank account information, to anyone. If you stop talking on dating sites, use an alternate email or phone number that isn't linked to your personal information. Don't send anyone money until you have known them for a year. Video chat to make sure they are real.

How do you know if you are being scammed on a dating site?

They don't want to meet in person. A scammer will ask for money for an emergency, such as a loved one dying. They fall in love soon. Another red flag is them quickly wanting to move off of a dating site to talk via text or email. If you think you're being scammed, report it and stop talking to them.

Summary

Have you ever fallen victim to an online romance scam? How did you find out? What would you add to the list to help other people avoid the same situation?

Do you feel like all you think about is him, but he only thinks about himself?

This doesn't mean he doesn't like you. You have to understand how he is wired. Once you do, you'll find there is a subtle thing you can say that to him that will drastically change how he shows his emotions towards you.

Don't forget to get those books I recommended to you in the introduction.

Thank you.

MY NOTES

Thank You

MY NOTES

Thank You

MY NOTES

Thank You

MY NOTES

Thank You

MY NOTES

Thank You

MY NOTES

Thank You

MY NOTES

Thank You

MY NOTES

Thank You

MY NOTES

Thank You

MY NOTES

....

....

....

....

....

....

....

....

....

Thank You

www.ingramcontent.com/pod-product-compliance
Lightning Source LLC
Chambersburg PA
CBHW070825170726
48000CB00019B/2748